Note: All activities in this book should be performed with
adult supervision. Common sense and care are essential to the
conduct of any and all activities, whether described in this book or not.
Neither the author nor the publisher assumes any responsibility
for any injuries or damages arising from any activities.

KINGFISHER
a Houghton Mifflin Company imprint
222 Berkeley Street
Boston, Massachusetts 02116
www.houghtonmifflinbooks.com

First published in 2005
2 4 6 8 10 9 7 5 3 1

Text copyright © Kingfisher 2005
Illustrations copyright © Jessie Eckel 2005
Created and produced by The Complete Works
St. Mary's Road, Royal Leamington Spa, Warwickshire, CV31 1JP U.K.

LIBRARY OF CONGRESS CATALOGING-IN-PUBLICATION DATA
has been applied for.

ISBN 0-7534-5921-3
ISBN 978-07534-5921-8

Printed in China
1TR/0605/SNPEXL/MA(MA)/128MA/F

How to be a Princess

in 7 days or less

Illustrated by Jessie Eckel

Text by Lesley Rees

KINGFISHER

BOSTON

Calling All Princesses!

Hi, I'm Princess Emily. Do you want to be a princess just like me?
Well, I can show you how! I'm going to give you a complete princess
makeover in only seven days, and we'll end up with an awesome party to celebrate.
So read on, girls—it's easier than you think!

I live in a palace with my royal family. There's my
mom (who's the queen, of course) and my dad
(you've guessed it, the king). Dad spends all day
watching out for wicked witches and fiery
dragons (yeah, right, what century is he
living in?). My baby sister, Chloe, is a
P.I.T.—that stands for Princess In Training!

When I grow up, I guess I'll be the
queen—how cool is that? But
in the meantime, I'm happy
just being me.

my bedroom

Chloe's bedroom

gardener

chef

maid

Mom

Dad

Chloe

me

lady-in-waiting

Sparkle

Any girl can be a princess. She doesn't have to live in a castle or a palace—princesses can live anywhere. Remember Rapunzel? She lived in a tiny room at the top of a tall tower, with nothing to do all day long but braid her hair.

braid

braid

sweep

sweep

And Snow White lived in a little cottage in the middle of a forest, sweeping and baking and cleaning for the seven dwarfs.

Tiara tips

Fashion fun

Beauty make & do

Bedroom D.I.Y.

So, as you can see, where you live isn't important. But what you *do* need is a really cool bedroom, a fabulous sense of style, and, most importantly, the right attitude. Luckily, I'm here to show you how to get them!

Get Decorating, Girls!

Day 1

Okay, princesses, today is D Day (that's "D" for "Decorating").
You might not live in a ritzy palace with a gazillion rooms, but
you can still give your bedroom a royal makeover. Just be sure
to get the king and queen's permission before you get going!

My bedroom is very princessy and pink. But it's not just
one shade of pink—I used lots of different pinks.

Prince Charming

Why not put a "throw"
over your bed or a chair?

Remember, darker colors make
rooms look smaller.

It's so easy to give your room a quick
makeover—just change the color of your
bedspread, curtains, or pillows.

I have pretty white curtains and lots of purple
and silver cushions on my bed—plus my teddy bear.
Well, a princess needs someone to confide in and cuddle!

All princesses need their beauty sleep!

Hanging a canopy over your bed will make you feel just like Sleeping Beauty.

Mirror, mirror on the wall, who has the best bedroom of them all?

A dressing table is a great place to keep your jewelry box and sparkly nail polish. If you don't have a dressing table, don't worry—a small bedside table or shelf will be just fine.

A princess can never have too many clothes!

If you don't have much space, try putting as many of your clothes and shoes away in a closet as you can—your room will look bigger, and you'll make the queen happy at the same time!

Above all, a princess's bedroom should reflect who she is. Even if you share your room, you can create a special space that showcases your personality and highlights your great taste.

Sparkly Surprises

Today we're going to make your fab bedroom look even better. You'll find everything you need to make these fun projects in the royal kitchen. They're guaranteed to make your room fit for a princess!

— You've Been Framed —

First of all, take . . .

- ♥ an empty cereal box
- ♥ scissors
- ♥ glue
- ♥ paint & a paintbrush
- ♥ dry macaroni
- ♥ glitter
- ♥ two photos

What you do next . . .

1. Take the cereal box and carefully cut off the top, sides, and bottom.

2. Fold the front in half widthwise—the plain side should face the outside, with the fold at the top.

Glue here.

3. Open this up and put glue on the inside.

4. Now fold it up again and firmly press together until it's stuck.

5. When the glue has dried, fold the cardboard in half lengthwise and then open it up. It should stand up like an open book.

6. Paint both sides of the cardboard in your favorite colors and leave it to dry.

7. Paint pieces of macaroni in pretty colors and sprinkle on glitter while they're still wet. Leave them to dry.

8. Next take two photos and carefully spread a little glue onto the back of each one. Place a photo on each side of the cardboard and press down gently.

9. Now glue the painted macaroni around the photos to decorate your new frame.

I made a frame for my fave pics of Prince Charming and Sparkle.

The Princess Is In

Now let's make a sign to hang over your bedroom doorknob to tell everyone whether you're in or out. You'll need all of the things that you used to make your photo frame, plus a cup, a pencil, and some pens.

What you do next . . .

1. Take a cereal box and cut off the front and back so that you have two large pieces of cardboard.

2. Take the front or back and fold it in half lengthwise. The plain side of the cardboard should face you, and the fold should be on the left.

3. Take a cup and place it on the cardboard, making sure that it's centered and around one inch down from the top.

4. Trace around the cup so that you have a circle shape.

5. Open up the cardboard and put glue on the inside.

6. Fold the cardboard back over again, pressing firmly to stick both sides together.

7. Carefully cut out the circle, making sure that you cut through both layers of cardboard. You may need an adult to help you do this.

8. Paint both sides and leave to dry.

9. On one side of the sign write "HRH (your name) IS IN!"

10. On the other side write "HRH (your name) IS OUT!"

11. Then decorate both sides with glitter and stickers and hang over your doorknob. You're now ready to receive guests—or go out!

glue glue

"HRH" means "Her Royal Highness."

ring ring

HRH EMILY IS OUT!

A Princess Party

Day 3

Princesses just want to have fun, and what could be more fun than throwing a party? By the end of this week you'll "graduate" from being a P.I.T. to a real princess. So why not celebrate by hosting a party for all of your princess pals?

Perfect Party Invitations

Remember how excited Cinderella was when her invitation to the ball arrived? Getting a party invitation is a thrill—sending one is too.

First of all, take . . .

- ♥ an empty cereal box
- ♥ colored pens
- ♥ scissors
- ♥ paper
- ♥ glitter
- ♥ stickers

What you do next . . .

1. Find a cereal box and draw a tiara shape onto it. Take a look at the tiara that came with this book to get an idea of the shape.

2. Cut out the tiara and use it as a template.

3. Place the template onto a sheet of paper and trace around it. Repeat to make several tiara shapes.

4. Cut out the tiara shapes.

5. Now write out the invitations. They could say something like . . .

> Princess (your name)
> Requests the pleasure of Princess
> (your friend's name)
> At a princess party
> On (put the party date here)
> At (put the party time and place here)
> Don't forget to wear your tiara!
> RSVP (add your phone number)

6. Finally, decorate with colored pens, glitter, and stickers. Now you can give or mail them to all of your princess friends.

RSVP is French for "please respond."

You can invite a few handsome princes if you want. But they can be a little bit greedy, so make sure that your servants guard the cakes.

Yum, yum!

Boys!

Don't forget to be home by midnight!

dance

dance

Sleeping Beauty had to wait a long time for her chance to have a party—100 years! Luckily, you only have to wait four more days.

Cinderella had so much fun at her party dancing with Prince Charming. But when the clock struck midnight, she had to run!

Only 91 years to go!

The Sparkly Stuff

Now, girls, it's time for us to check out the sparkly stuff!
Do you have a huge collection of necklaces, rings, and earrings?
A true princess can never have too much jewelry. Of course, you can't
wear all of your shiny gems at once, so here's where you can keep them.

Emily's Jewelry Box

First of all, take . . .

- ♥ glue
- ♥ paint
- ♥ a paintbrush
- ♥ glitter
- ♥ stickers/jewels

- ♥ an old shoe box
  or ice-cream carton
- ♥ 4 plastic lids from
  cans of hair spray or
  furniture polish

What you do next . . .

1. Pour some of the glue into a container. Add the paint, drop by drop, and mix using the paintbrush until you get the color that you want.

2. Sprinkle in some glitter.

3. Now paint the glue mixture all over your shoe box or carton, both inside and outside, as well as on both sides of the lid. When it's dry, the glue will make the box look shiny, and the glitter will make it sparkle.

4. When your shoe box or carton is dry, paint the top of your plastic lids with plain glue and stick them down in each corner of your box to make little cups. These will be perfect for holding rings and earrings.

5. Finally, decorate with some of your glitter stickers or stick-on jewels.

Now you can fill your jewelry box with all of your trinkets, bracelets, and chains. Why not make one as a gift for the queen or for one of your princess pals?

glitter

glitter

Try not to touch the back of your jewels so that they stay sticky.

If your new jewelry box is looking a little empty, just use the jewel earrings that came with this book for instant sparkle. Simply peel a jewel off the paper and position it on your earlobe. Press it gently to hold it in place. Pick earrings that match your clothes or your eye color.

Princess Tresses

The next step to becoming a princess is good hair care. Rapunzel kept her long locks in tip-top condition, which was handy when her handsome prince needed a ladder to climb up! You can use the hair bands that came with this book to try out these princessy styles.

Bouncy Braid

If your hair is long, an easy way to keep it looking neat is to braid it.

1. Brush all of your hair to the back of your head and gather it up at your neck.

2. Now divide it into three sections—like this, okay?

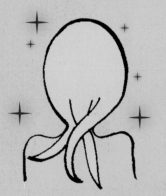

3. Take the right section and cross it over the middle section. See how the right section has now become the middle section?

4. Then take the left section and cross it over the middle section.

5. Then cross the right section over the middle section so that it becomes the middle section once again.

6. Keep going until all of your hair is in one long braid and then hold it together with a hair band.

7. Now tie a ribbon around the end of your braid and pull the braid upward. The braid forms a loop, with the end underneath.

8. Take the ribbon up on either side of the braid and tie in a bow over the top.

It might seem hard at first, but remember: every time you cross a left or right section over the middle section, it becomes the new middle. If you keep practicing, you'll quickly get the hang of it.

Twirl Time

Princess Morgan loves to style her shoulder-length tresses with pretty hair clips.

1. First of all, brush your hair. Then take a small section and twirl it around and around until it looks like a small rope.

2. Pull the "rope" sideways or backward tightly and use a hair clip to attach the end of the "rope" to the rest of your hair.

3. Now take another section of hair next to it and do it all over again. This is a really good way of tying back your bangs or the sides of your hair.

Short 'n' Sweet

Princesses with short hair have so many style options. Here are just a few great party hairdos.

1. Take a small bunch of hair in one hand and a hair band in the other hand.

2. Pull the elastic over the hair and push it to the base of the bunch. Twist and pull it over again until it's tight enough to hold your hair in place. Repeat until all of your hair is in bunches.

Princess Courtney looks so glamorous with her hair in tiny bunches.

Princess Britney loves using sparkly hair gel to "mold" her hair into spikes.

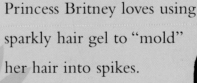

Princess Chelsea likes to slick back her hair with wet-look gel so that it lies sleek and flat on her head. She always pulls down a piece of her bangs and gels it into a tiny curl.

Looking Good, Girls!

Day 5

Because they always try to look their best, princesses need lots of clothes. You might not have a fairy godmother to wave a magic wand over you or lots of mice to help you get dressed, but you've got me! Let's see what outfits you should wear for different occasions.

A beautiful long dress and a tiara is the perfect outfit to wear to Prince Charming's ball.

Whoops!

Long dresses require poise and practice—oh no!

I'm not looking!

It's a wrap!

It's time for tea with the Queen Mom. A short dress or a pretty skirt and top is just right. I always throw a wrap around my shoulders— it dresses up any outfit, even my jeans.

Tankini or bikini?

Sarongs are hip.

I love going to the beach and
hanging out with my friends.
Remember to pack the sunscreen!

When I've finished soaking up the sun, I like
to hit the stores in a pair of shorts and a T-shirt.
Any color is fine—but I usually go for pink.
Cool sunglasses complete my look!

SPARKLE CITY

*Use a scarf as a
belt—very princessy!*

Shop till you drop!

Choices, choices!

Accessories are a great way
to give old clothes a new twist.
The right purse, belt, hat, and
shoes can really make an outfit.

So, what should you wear to
your party? Whatever makes you
feel good—it's your party, after all!

Royal Etiquette

Your tiara and impeccable manners show everyone that you're a princess. Your tiara is not just for formal occasions; you can wear it almost anywhere—except when you're in bed or washing your hair, of course! Here's a handy guide to when you should and shouldn't wear your tiara.

Riding lesson: It doesn't fit over the helmet!

To a party: Any party, any time!

Gym class: It can make doing a headstand a little bit painful!

Doing homework: It helps me think.

Swimming: Okay for pool parties, not so good for scuba diving!

To the movies: Yes—it might be a premiere.

Wearing your tiara should make you feel like a princess, so you'd better behave like one. Getting into a car should be elegant—not a scramble.

1. First get your chauffeur to open the door.
2. Facing outward, sink slowly down onto the seat—no collapsing!

3. Then swivel around, bending both legs at the same time with your ankles together, and lift your legs into the car.
4. Sit up straight with your hands on your lap. Now you're ready to go!

See, it's easy.

Princesses also need to know how to wave properly. You should greet your subjects with an elegant and graceful motion—not like you're trying to direct traffic!

dab
dab

A princess should have perfect table manners. She never chews with her mouth open (yuck, how gross would that be?). Unlike some princes, she always uses her napkin and not her sleeve to wipe her mouth. Most importantly, she never forgets to say "please" and "thank you."

Princess Party Food

The invitations have gone out and you know what you're wearing, but what are you going to feed your party guests? A true princess doesn't want to spend hours working in the kitchen, so here are some quick and delicious recipes to prepare in advance.

Princess Punch

First of all, take . . .

- ♥ lemon-flavored soda
- ♥ a large pitcher
- ♥ strawberry- or cherry-flavored drink powder
- ♥ a plastic knife
- ♥ apples
- ♥ grapes
- ♥ strawberries
- ♥ ice cubes
- ♥ glasses

Sparkle! Fizz! Pop!

What you do next . . .

1. Pour the lemon soda into a pitcher.

2. Add some strawberry- or cherry-flavored drink powder and stir until it's the perfect shade of pink.

3. Carefully chop the apples into chunks.

4. Put the apple chunks, grapes, and strawberries into the pitcher and add ice cubes.

5. Serve in pretty glasses, making sure that everyone gets some fruit.

Tasty and healthy!

— Sparkly Cookies —

First of all, take . . .

- a spoon
- powdered sugar
- a bowl
- water
- red food coloring
- sugar cookies
- a plate
- sprinkles & edible silver balls

What you do next . . .

1. Spoon some powdered sugar into a clean bowl and add some water.

2. Mix until smooth. Don't worry if the mixture looks too thin—just add a little more powdered sugar and stir. If it's too thick, just add a little more water. The mixture should coat the back of your spoon and drip off easily.

3. Now add red food coloring, one drop at a time, until it's the perfect shade of pink.

4. Drizzle some pink frosting over each cookie.

5. Place the cookies on a plate and shake on the sprinkles and silver balls.

6. Refrigerate until the frosting has set.

Why not put your friends' initials on the cookies?

— Cheesy Delights —

First of all, take . . .

- a plastic knife
- some Cheddar cheese
- wooden skewers
- grapes
- an orange (cut in half)
- a plate

What you do next . . .

1. Cut the Cheddar cheese into chunks.

2. Take a wooden skewer and, carefully holding it at one end, push a grape onto it.

3. Now take a chunk of cheese and push that onto the skewer too.

4. Take another grape and pop it on the top.

5. Now push the skewer into half an orange and start all over again.

Easy and cheesy!

Yum Yum

You could use other fruits if you prefer—like pineapple or mango chunks. Just be careful when you're cutting them up, okay?

Party Games

Just one day to go until you can eat all of that yummy food, twirl around in your best party dress, and play all kinds of cool games. In case you don't know what party games princesses like to play, here are a few fun ideas.

— Kiss the Frog —

Draw a big frog on a piece of paper and tape it to a wall. Each princess takes turns putting on lip gloss and a blindfold and then spins around three times before trying to kiss the frog on its lips. Each princess's name is written next to her "lip print," and the one who smooches Froggy on his big kissable lips is the winner!

Mmm, strawberry lip gloss—my fave!

Cinderella says . . . you're out!

— Cinderella Says —

Choose one person to be Cinderella. Cinderella is a princess, so she gives everyone commands like "Cinderella says . . . touch your tiara!" or "Cinderella says . . . curtsy!" Everyone must do as Cinderella commands. But if she doesn't say "Cinderella says . . .," you shouldn't do it—or you're out!

— Hunt the Poison Apple —

Hide mini candy bars and a red apple—like the one that the Wicked Queen gave to Snow White—around your house. Ask your princess guests to hunt for them. When someone finds a candy bar, she can eat it. The real winner is the one who finds the apple, which can be exchanged for a prize.

Gotcha!

Choc-o-licious!

– Ditch the Witch –

Everyone sits in a circle, and one princess holds an apple. When the music starts, the princesses pass the apple around until the music is stopped. Then whomever is holding the apple isn't a princess—she's a wicked witch! Everyone shouts "Ditch the witch!," and that person is out. Start again and keep going until there's only one princess left.

Ditch the witch!

z
z z

Princess Pamper Time

At last, the big day has arrived, fellow princesses! It's time to get ready for your party. A princess should always smell as fresh as a daisy, even after a hard day at princess school. A relaxing bubble bath is a great way to pamper yourself.

I love tons of frothy bubbles. In fact, I have my very own bubble bath, which my little sister, Chloe, is not allowed to use! If you would like to make your own, here's how.

Rub-a-dub-dub, there's a princess in the tub!

Super-Easy Bubble Bath

First of all, take . . .

- ♥ an empty plastic bottle
- ♥ 1 cup of unscented shampoo
- ♥ 1 cup of water
- ♥ 1 teaspoon of salt
- ♥ essential oil
- ♥ 2 drops of red food coloring

What you do next . . .

1. Find an empty plastic bottle.

2. Pour in the shampoo.

3. Add the water and mix carefully.

4. Add the salt and stir it all up until it becomes thick.

5. Now add the essential oil (like vanilla, rose, or lemongrass), drop by drop, until it smells as strong as you want—don't put too much in at once, though.

Mix it up and make it nice!

6. Add the red food coloring one drop at a time. Mix until it's pink.

7. Finally, tie a pretty ribbon around the top, and voilà—your very own princess bubble bath is ready!

You can use your sparkly stickers to decorate the bottle. Now all you have to do is pour some of your bubble bath into the tub while the water is running, and you'll have lots of relaxing bubbles.

Now it's time to get dressed for the party!

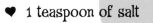

You've Made It!

Wow, wasn't that just the busiest week ever? But all of your hard work was worth it. You've made it to your graduation party, and you're now officially a princess. Congratulations! Remember, a princess's work is never done. We have high standards to maintain!

Now that I've taught you how to be a princess, it's up to you to keep the spirit alive. Being a true princess is about being beautiful on the inside, as well as on the outside. A princess is nice to her parents, thoughtful to her friends, polite to her teachers, and kind to animals.

A true princess stands out from the crowd because, deep down, she knows that wherever she is and whatever she's doing, she's just lucky to be herself.

Princesses rule—okay!

Enough of the serious stuff! What every true princess *also* knows is that a girl can never have too many gorgeous dresses and jewels. As for a tiara, well, what can I tell you? It's part of the uniform! Right, girls?

Anyway, thanks for letting me share my secrets with you. It's been fun. Bye, princesses— keep sparkling!

PRINCESS EMILY'S RULES

Think princess!

1. A princess can never have too many beautiful clothes or shoes.
2. Don't forget to wear your tiara.
3. Princesses are always polite.
4. Always treat the king and queen with respect.
5. Princesses love presents—but always remember to say "thank you."
6. Princesses should smell as pretty as they look, so hit that shower, girls.
7. Someday your prince will come—believe me.
8. A smile is a princess's most dazzling accessory.
9. We are all princesses on the inside.
10. Think princess—and you'll be one!